The Hercules Myth

Douglas Albert Amos

Published by Douglas Amos, 2024.

THE HERCULES MYTH

First edition. November 1, 2024.

Copyright © 2024 Douglas Albert Amos.

ISBN: 979-8227783394

Written by Douglas Albert Amos.

Also by Douglas Albert Amos

The Myth of Hercules

Chapter 1: The Myth of Hercules and His Twelve Labors

The Origins of Hercules

The origins of Hercules are steeped in rich stories of mythology that intertwines with the ancient Greek worldview. Born as the son of Zeus, the king of the gods, and Alcmene, a mortal woman, Hercules embodies the duality of divine and human nature. His birth was marked by extraordinary circumstances, including Zeus's deceptive transformation to seduce Alcmene. This union not only illustrated the complexity of divine relationships in mythology but also set the stage for Hercules' lifelong struggle against both mortal and divine adversities. The narrative of his conception and birth serves as a prologue to the epic tales that define his character, showcasing the inherent conflict between human vulnerability and divine power.

Hercules' early life was fraught with challenges, a theme that resonates throughout his mythos. As an infant, he displayed immense strength, famously slaying two serpents sent by Hera, Zeus's wife, who was jealous of her husband's infidelity. This event foreshadows the trials Hercules would face as an adult, as much of his life became a battleground for overcoming obstacles. The serpents symbolize the external threats that Hercules must confront, often rooted in the jealousy and wrath of the gods, particularly Hera, who became a recurring antagonist in his life. The nature of these challenges reflects the broader theme of struggle against forces beyond one's control, a concept that resonates in various mythologies around the world.

The Twelve Labors of Hercules, a series of seemingly insurmountable tasks, were a direct result of Hera's relentless pursuit of vengeance against him. Each labor, from slaying the Nemean Lion to capturing the Golden

Hind, serves as a symbolic representation of internal and external conflicts. These tasks are not merely physical challenges; they encapsulate psychological struggles that reflect Hercules' journey toward self-discovery and redemption. The myth of Hercules can be viewed through the lens of personal growth, where each labor represents a stage of development, allowing for a deeper understanding of one's strengths and weaknesses. This aspect of his story aligns with the archetypal hero's journey, where transformation often stems from overcoming adversity.

In examining the role of women in Hercules' narrative, it is essential to consider the impact of figures such as Alcmene and Hera. Alcmene, as Hercules' mother, represents the nurturing aspect of femininity, while Hera embodies the vengeful and jealous archetype. The contrasting portrayals of women in Hercules' life highlight the complexities of gender dynamics within Greek mythology. The motivations and actions of these female characters reflect societal attitudes toward women in ancient Greece, offering a platform to explore feminist perspectives on power, agency, and influence. Their roles are integral to the development of Hercules' story, as they shape his trials and ultimately contribute to his growth.

The legacy of Hercules extends beyond ancient Greece, influencing various cultures and modern interpretations. His story has been reimagined in literature, film, and art, showcasing the timeless appeal of the hero archetype. The symbolic struggles of Hercules resonate with contemporary audiences, as they reflect universal themes of perseverance, strength, and the quest for identity. By exploring the origins of Hercules and the complexities of his character, we gain insights into the values and ethics that continue to shape our understanding of heroism today. The tale of Hercules invites readers to reflect on their own struggles and the paths they choose in overcoming adversity, making it a relevant narrative across generations.

Overview of the Twelve Labors

The Twelve Labors of Hercules represent a series of heroic feats that the demigod Hercules undertook as a means of atonement for a grave mistake driven by madness, sent upon him by the goddess Hera. This mythological narrative serves not only as an engaging tale of adventure but also as a profound exploration of human struggle and redemption. Each labor is emblematic of different challenges and personal growth, reflecting the universal themes of perseverance and resilience. These tasks, ranging from slaying the Nemean Lion to retrieving the Golden Apples of the Hesperides, illustrate not just physical strength but also mental fortitude and moral integrity.

The labors are steeped in rich symbolism, with each task representing specific life challenges that resonate with audiences across cultures and eras. For instance, the Nemean Lion symbolizes the confrontation of seemingly insurmountable obstacles, while the capturing of the Ceryneian Hind reflects the pursuit of elusive goals. As Hercules faces each labor, he embodies the archetypal hero, grappling with internal and external conflicts that mirror the struggles faced by individuals in their own lives. This aspect of the myth invites readers to reflect on their personal journeys and the adversities they encounter.

In analyzing the Twelve Labors through a feminist lens, one can observe the often-overlooked roles of female figures within the narrative. Characters such as Hera, who instigates Hercules' trials, and the various goddesses who assist or challenge him, provide critical insights into the dynamics of power and agency. The portrayal of women in these myths raises questions about their influence and representation in a predominantly male-dominated heroic framework. This perspective encourages a deeper understanding of gender roles in mythology and the implications they have on contemporary discussions regarding strength and vulnerability.

The historical context of the Hercules myth reveals its roots in ancient Greek culture, where the stories served not only as entertainment but also as moral lessons. The Twelve Labors were likely influenced by the societal values of bravery, honor, and the importance of divine favor. As Hercules navigates these trials, he not only seeks personal redemption but also upholds the ideals of heroism prevalent in ancient Greek society. This historical backdrop enriches the narrative, offering insights into how the character of Hercules has evolved over time and the ways in which his story has been adapted and retold.

Finally, the influence of Hercules extends beyond ancient texts into modern pop culture, where his legacy continues to shape narratives of heroism. From films to literature, the archetype of the hero facing insurmountable odds is prevalent, illustrating the timeless appeal of Hercules' story. The Twelve Labors serve as a framework for understanding not only the struggles of Hercules but also the broader human experience. By decoding these labors, readers can uncover valuable lessons about overcoming adversity, the complexities of personal growth, and the enduring power of myth in shaping cultural values and ethics.

Significance of Hercules in Greek Mythology

Hercules, known as Heracles in Greek mythology, stands as one of the most significant figures in ancient lore, embodying the ideals of strength, heroism, and perseverance. His narrative offers rich insights into the human experience, showcasing the struggles and triumphs that define the human condition. The tales of Hercules, particularly the Twelve Labors, serve as a framework for understanding not only personal challenges but also the broader societal values of ancient Greece. Through his legendary feats, Hercules becomes a symbol of the archetypal hero, representing the journey of self-discovery and the pursuit of virtue amidst adversity.

The Twelve Labors of Hercules are not merely a series of daunting tasks but rather symbolic trials that reflect various aspects of human struggle and growth. Each labor presents a unique challenge that Hercules must confront, from slaying the Nemean Lion to capturing the Golden Hind. These tasks illustrate the themes of courage, resilience, and the necessity of facing one's fears. In this way, Hercules serves as a model for overcoming obstacles and achieving personal transformation, making his story relevant across different cultures and time periods. The symbolic nature of these labors resonates with anyone embarking on their own path of self-improvement and growth.

In comparative mythology, Hercules shares similarities with other heroic figures around the world, such as Gilgamesh, Beowulf, and the Indian hero Rama. These characters often encounter trials that test their strength and moral fortitude, highlighting universal themes of heroism and the quest for identity. The parallels between Hercules and these figures suggest a shared cultural narrative that spans various civilizations, illustrating how societies encode their values and ideals through myth. This comparative analysis enriches our understanding of what it means to be a hero and how these archetypes shape our perceptions of courage and virtue.

Feminist perspectives on Hercules' adventures also offer a critical lens through which to examine the role of women in his narrative. While Hercules is often celebrated for his strength and bravery, the stories frequently feature powerful female figures, such as Hera, who plays a pivotal role in his trials. These women, though sometimes depicted as antagonists, embody complex traits that challenge traditional gender roles. By analyzing the interactions between Hercules and these women, we gain insight into the societal views of gender in ancient Greece and how these perspectives continue to influence modern interpretations of heroism.

Lastly, the legacy of Hercules extends beyond ancient texts into contemporary culture, where he is often reimagined in films, literature, and other media. This ongoing fascination with Hercules underscores his enduring appeal as a symbol of strength and resilience. The challenges he faces resonate with modern audiences, who can relate to the theme of overcoming adversity. By exploring Hercules' impact on popular culture, we can appreciate how ancient myths adapt and thrive, continuing to shape contemporary values and ethics while providing timeless lessons about the human spirit.

Chapter 2: Comparative Mythology: Hercules and Similar Heroes

Heroes Across Cultures

Throughout history, cultures around the world have produced their own heroic figures who embody strength, bravery, and the quest for justice. These heroes often reflect the values and ideals of their societies, serving as symbols of hope and resilience in the face of adversity. While Hercules remains one of the most iconic heroes of ancient mythology, many cultures have developed their own legends with striking similarities to his Twelve Labors. From the epic tales of Gilgamesh in Mesopotamia to the heroic deeds of Beowulf in Northern Europe, these figures demonstrate the universal human experience of struggle and triumph.

In comparing Hercules to other cultural heroes, one can observe common themes that resonate across different mythologies. For example, the hero's journey often involves a series of challenges that test their strength, intellect, and moral character. In the case of Hercules, his Twelve Labors serve as a rite of passage, marking his transformation from a flawed individual into a revered hero. Similarly, in the Epic of Gilgamesh, the protagonist embarks on quests that not only challenge him physically but also force him to confront existential questions about mortality and friendship. These narratives reveal the archetypal journey of the hero, showcasing the trials that shape their identities and destinies.

The role of women in these myths is also significant, often reflecting societal attitudes toward gender. In Hercules' labors, female figures such as Hera and the Amazons play critical roles, either as antagonists or as symbols of strength. This dynamic is echoed in other myths, where female characters are portrayed as both powerful and complex. For instance, the goddess Inanna in Sumerian mythology challenges the status quo and embodies themes of empowerment. Examining these representations helps to highlight the evolving perspectives on femininity and strength throughout various cultures, emphasizing the importance of women's contributions to heroic narratives.

From a psychological perspective, the struggles faced by heroes like Hercules can be interpreted as symbolic representations of the inner conflicts individuals face in their own lives. The Twelve Labors can be seen as metaphors for personal growth, illustrating the journey toward self-actualization. In this light, Hercules' challenges resonate with the audience, encouraging them to confront their own trials and emerge stronger. This psychological analysis of heroism invites readers to reflect on their own experiences, fostering a deeper understanding of the universal human condition.

Ultimately, the legacy of Hercules and similar heroes across cultures serves as a testament to the enduring power of myth. These stories not only entertain but also offer moral lessons and reflections on human nature. As modern society continues to grapple with its own challenges, the tales of Hercules and other heroes provide inspiration and guidance. By exploring the stories of global mythology, one can gain insights into the shared values that unite us, illustrating that while the details of heroic narratives may differ, the essence of the hero remains a crucial part of the human experience.

Comparison with Gilgamesh

The epic narratives of Hercules and Gilgamesh, two iconic figures from distinct ancient civilizations, reveal profound similarities and differences in their respective journeys. Both heroes undertake monumental quests that challenge their physical and psychological limits, serving as reflections of their cultures' values. Hercules, rooted in Greek mythology, exemplifies the heroic ideal of strength and perseverance, while Gilgamesh, from Mesopotamian lore, embodies the quest for immortality and the search for meaning in life. By comparing these two myths, we can gain a deeper understanding of their symbolic struggles and the archetypal themes that resonate across time and cultures.

Hercules is often celebrated for his twelve labors, which symbolize the triumph of the human spirit over insurmountable odds. Each labor presents unique challenges that require not only strength but also cunning and resilience. In contrast, Gilgamesh's journey is marked by his quest for eternal life following the death of his friend Enkidu. This pursuit leads him to encounter various deities and mythical creatures, ultimately teaching him lessons about mortality and the importance of human connections. While Hercules's labors focus on external challenges, Gilgamesh's story emphasizes internal growth and the acceptance of human limitations.

The roles of divine intervention in the narratives also present a point of comparison. In Hercules's story, the gods frequently intervene, offering assistance or creating obstacles, reflecting the Greek belief in fate and the influence of the divine on human affairs. Similarly, Gilgamesh encounters gods who guide or hinder him, but his journey is more introspective, emphasizing the relationship between divine beings and humanity. The presence of divine forces in both myths highlights the complex interplay between human agency and external power, showcasing how these themes manifest differently in both narratives.

Feminist perspectives on these myths further enrich the comparison. In Hercules's labors, women often play pivotal roles, either as adversaries or catalysts for his actions. Figures like Hera and the Amazonian queen Hippolyta present challenges that reveal the complexities of gender dynamics in Greek society. Conversely, Gilgamesh's story features significant female characters, such as the goddess Ishtar and Siduri, the tavern keeper, who provide wisdom and guidance, emphasizing the importance of female agency. The treatment of women in both myths offers insights into the societal attitudes of their respective cultures, highlighting the evolving roles of women in mythology.

Ultimately, the legacies of Hercules and Gilgamesh extend far beyond their ancient origins. Both figures continue to inspire modern interpretations in literature, film, and popular culture, symbolizing the timeless struggles of humanity. Their stories encapsulate essential themes of strength, mortality, and the pursuit of purpose, resonating with contemporary values and ethics. As we examine these myths through various lenses, including comparative mythology and psychological analysis, we uncover the enduring relevance of Hercules and Gilgamesh, reminding us that the struggles they faced are not unlike those we encounter today.

The Hero's Journey in Different Traditions

The concept of the hero's journey is a universal theme that transcends cultures and time periods, manifesting in various mythologies around the world. In the context of Hercules and his Twelve Labors, this archetypal narrative resonates not only within Greek mythology but also in numerous global stories. From the epic tales of Gilgamesh in Mesopotamia to the adventures of Krishna in Hindu tradition, the hero's journey often involves a call to adventure, trials that test the hero's strength and character, and eventual transformation. These common threads highlight the shared human experience of facing challenges and striving for personal growth.

In many traditions, heroes embark on quests that symbolize the struggle against chaos and the pursuit of order. For instance, in the Hindu epic Mahabharata, Arjuna faces moral dilemmas and battles that parallel Hercules' physical confrontations with monstrous foes. Both heroes undergo significant personal development, learning valuable lessons about duty, sacrifice, and the nature of courage. The cyclical nature of their journeys—moving from challenges to victories and ultimately to a deeper understanding of themselves—serves as a reminder of the inherent struggles in life, making their tales relevant to audiences across generations.

The role of divine intervention is another notable aspect of the hero's journey seen in various traditions. In Hercules' case, the gods play a crucial role in both his trials and his eventual redemption. Similarly, in the African folklore of Anansi the Spider, the trickster figures often receive help from supernatural beings to navigate their challenges. This divine assistance emphasizes the interconnectedness of human efforts and the influence of higher powers in overcoming adversity. Such narratives encourage individuals to seek guidance and remain open to support from others, whether from divine sources or their communities.

Feminist perspectives also enrich the discussion of the hero's journey by highlighting the roles of women in these narratives. In many cultures, female figures serve as either obstacles or guides, shaping the hero's path. For example, in the story of Hercules, figures like Hera and Atalanta present both challenges and support, reflecting the complex dynamics of gender in heroism. This exploration reveals the necessity of acknowledging women's contributions and experiences in mythological narratives, offering a more nuanced understanding of the journey toward heroism.

Ultimately, the hero's journey in various traditions serves as a powerful framework for understanding not only the adventures of Hercules but also the collective human experience. By examining the commonalities and differences in these narratives, we glean insights into the values and ethics that shape our societies. The enduring legacy of these myths continues to influence modern culture, reminding us that the struggles inherent in the hero's journey are timeless and resonate across diverse contexts, encouraging personal growth and resilience in the face of adversity.

Chapter 3: Psychological Analysis of Hercules

Archetypes in Mythology

Archetypes in mythology serve as universal symbols that resonate across cultures and time periods, representing fundamental human experiences and emotions. In the context of Hercules and his Twelve Labors, these archetypes play a crucial role in illustrating the hero's journey and the challenges he faces. The archetypal hero is often characterized by attributes such as strength, bravery, and perseverance. Hercules embodies these traits, but he also grapples with inner conflicts and moral dilemmas, making him a complex figure that reflects the struggles of humanity.

One prominent archetype found in Hercules' story is that of the Hero. This archetype is not only about physical strength but also involves the hero's quest for identity and purpose. Hercules' labors symbolize a rite of passage, where he confronts external challenges while also wrestling with his internal demons. Each labor serves as a metaphor for personal growth, highlighting the importance of resilience and the transformative power of overcoming adversity. This duality of external and internal struggles resonates with audiences and allows them to see aspects of their own lives reflected in Hercules' journey.

Another significant archetype present in the myth is the Mentor, often represented by figures like Athena and Chiron. These characters provide guidance and wisdom, helping Hercules navigate his path. The Mentor archetype emphasizes the importance of learning and growth through mentorship, suggesting that heroes do not operate in isolation. Instead, their journeys are enriched by the knowledge and support of others. This dynamic showcases the interconnectedness of individuals within a community and the value of seeking help when facing challenges.

The archetype of the Shadow is also prevalent in Hercules' narrative, represented by the monsters and obstacles he must overcome. Each labor, from slaying the Nemean Lion to capturing the Golden Hind, symbolizes not only a physical confrontation but also a confrontation with darker aspects of the self. This archetypal struggle illustrates the necessity of facing one's fears and weaknesses, reinforcing the idea that true heroism involves personal introspection and growth. By vanquishing these shadows, Hercules not only proves his external strength but also achieves a deeper understanding of himself.

Finally, the archetype of the Feminine emerges through the portrayal of various female figures in Hercules' story, such as Hera, Megara, and the Amazons. These characters often embody complex roles, reflecting societal views on femininity and strength. Their interactions with Hercules challenge traditional gender roles and highlight the importance of female agency in the narrative. By examining these archetypes, readers can appreciate the multifaceted nature of the myth, recognizing that the struggles and triumphs of Hercules are intertwined with the experiences of women, thereby enriching the overall story of the mythological narrative.

Personal Growth Through Struggle

Personal growth often emerges from the most challenging struggles, and this principle is vividly illustrated through the Twelve Labors of Hercules. Each labor represents not only a formidable task but also a pivotal moment in Hercules' journey toward self-discovery and maturation. The trials he faces are not merely external challenges; they mirror the inner conflicts and growth that occur when individuals confront their limitations. By examining these labors, we can uncover the deeper significance behind each struggle and how they contribute to Hercules' evolution as a hero.

The first labor, the Nemean Lion, embodies the struggle against seemingly insurmountable odds. Hercules learns to confront his fears and insecurities by facing a creature that is invulnerable to ordinary weapons. This labor symbolizes the necessity of resilience and adaptation in overcoming obstacles. It teaches that true strength lies not just in physical prowess but in the ability to confront and adapt to challenges, a lesson that resonates with anyone navigating their own personal struggles.

As Hercules progresses through his labors, the tasks become increasingly complex and symbolic. The capture of the Golden Hind, for instance, represents the pursuit of elusive goals and the importance of patience and strategy. In this labor, Hercules must balance the urgency of his quest with the need for respect towards the creature he is tasked with capturing. This duality reflects the tension between ambition and ethics, encouraging individuals to consider the impact of their actions on the world around them as they strive for personal success.

Moreover, the Labors of Hercules also highlight the importance of support systems and relationships in the journey of personal growth. The involvement of various deities and mentors throughout his trials illustrates the value of guidance and collaboration. Just as Hercules receives assistance from figures like Athena, we are reminded that seeking help from others can be crucial in overcoming our own struggles. This aspect emphasizes that personal growth is not a solitary endeavor; it often requires the strength and wisdom of others to navigate the complexities of life.

Ultimately, the Twelve Labors serve as a powerful metaphor for the transformative power of struggle. Each labor reveals layers of Hercules' character and illustrates that true heroism lies in the ability to face adversity with courage and integrity. As readers, we can draw parallels between Hercules' challenges and our own lives, recognizing that personal growth often arises from our struggles. These mythic tales encourage us to embrace our own labors, understanding that every challenge faced is an opportunity for profound self-discovery and growth.

The Hero's Internal Conflicts

The internal conflicts of Hercules serve as a pivotal aspect of his character and the narrative surrounding his Twelve Labors. At the heart of these struggles lies the tension between his divine heritage and his human vulnerabilities. As the son of Zeus, Hercules possesses immense strength and potential, yet he is continually faced with the limitations and flaws characteristic of humanity. This duality creates a rich internal dialogue, where he grapples with feelings of inadequacy, guilt, and the quest for identity. These conflicts are not merely background elements; they are integral to understanding Hercules as a hero who must navigate both external challenges and his own psyche.

One of the most prominent internal conflicts Hercules faces is the burden of his past actions, particularly the tragic incident where he unwittingly killed his wife and children in a fit of madness sent by Hera. This event catalyzes his journey of atonement, forcing him to confront his feelings of guilt and despair. Each labor he undertakes symbolizes not only a physical challenge but also a step toward redemption. The psychological weight of his past haunts him, illustrating the theme of personal responsibility and the struggle to overcome one's darker impulses. As he battles mythical beasts and completes seemingly impossible tasks, these external conflicts mirror his inner turmoil, showcasing a hero not just defined by his strength, but also by his capacity for growth and change.

Moreover, Hercules' relationship with the gods adds another layer to his internal conflicts. While he often receives divine assistance, he is also subject to their whims and jealousy. This complex interplay leads him to question his place in the world and the nature of his existence. Is he a mere pawn in the games of the gods, or does he possess agency over his fate? The struggle for autonomy against divine intervention becomes a central theme in his journey, reflecting the universal human quest for control in the face of external forces. This conflict resonates with audiences as it mirrors our own battles against circumstances beyond our control.

Hercules' internal conflicts also reflect broader themes of masculinity and vulnerability. In many interpretations of the myth, strength is often equated with stoicism and emotional suppression. However, Hercules' journey reveals that true strength lies in acknowledging one's fears and failures. His willingness to confront his inner demons challenges traditional notions of heroism, suggesting that vulnerability can coexist with bravery. This perspective opens up dialogue about the pressures placed on individuals, particularly men, to conform to rigid ideals of strength and toughness, emphasizing the importance of emotional intelligence and resilience.

Ultimately, Hercules' internal conflicts serve as a narrative device that not only enriches his character but also offers profound insights into the human condition. Through his struggles, audiences are invited to reflect on their own internal battles and the complexities of their identities. The myth of Hercules transcends mere physical feats; it encapsulates the essence of what it means to be human—an ongoing journey of self-discovery, redemption, and the pursuit of meaning in a world filled with challenges. As modern interpretations of Hercules continue to evolve, the exploration of his internal conflicts remains a vital element, highlighting the timeless relevance of his story in contemporary discourse on heroism and personal growth.

Chapter 4: Feminist Perspectives on Hercules

The Role of Women in Hercules' Labors

In the context of Hercules' labors, women play multifaceted roles that often reflect the complexities of their societal positions in ancient Greece. While Hercules himself is the central figure of strength and heroism, the influence and actions of female characters are pivotal in shaping his journey. The women encountered by Hercules, whether as allies, adversaries, or symbols of moral dilemmas, highlight the intricate dynamics of gender and power in mythology. Each labor not only showcases Hercules' physical prowess but also serves as a stage for examining the virtues and vices embodied by these women.

The first significant female figure in the labors is Hera, the queen of the gods, whose animosity toward Hercules is deeply rooted in her jealousy of Zeus' infidelity. Hera's role as an antagonist is crucial, as her relentless pursuit of Hercules through various trials illustrates the theme of divine opposition. This relationship exemplifies the intersection of gender and power, where female deities wield considerable influence over male heroes. Hera's actions reflect a broader commentary on the complexities of femininity, portraying women as both nurturing and vengeful, depending on their circumstances and relationships with men.

In addition to Hera, other women in Hercules' narrative serve as pivotal figures in his quest for redemption and strength. For example, the Nemean Lion's skin, which Hercules wears as a symbol of his strength, is also connected to the lioness, representing a fierce and protective femininity. Similarly, the encounter with the Amazons during his labors reveals a society of warrior women who challenge traditional gender roles. The Amazons embody empowerment and resistance, presenting a contrasting view of femininity that is strong and independent, further enriching the narrative of Hercules' struggles.

Moreover, the role of women in Hercules' labors extends into the realms of morality and sacrifice. Characters like Deianira, Hercules' wife, represent the emotional and ethical complexities faced by women in relationships with powerful men. Her tragic decision to use a love potion ultimately leads to Hercules' demise, symbolizing the consequences of love and jealousy. This highlights how women in the myth are not merely passive figures but active participants in the moral dilemmas that shape the hero's journey, emphasizing the duality of their roles as both nurturers and potential destroyers.

The portrayal of women in the Twelve Labors of Hercules invites a deeper examination of gender dynamics and societal values in ancient mythology. By analyzing these female characters, we can discern how their actions and fates contribute to the overarching themes of struggle and growth found in Hercules' narrative. This exploration not only enriches our understanding of the myth itself but also encourages contemporary reflections on the roles of women in stories of heroism, challenging readers to reconsider how gender influences the perception of strength and virtue in both ancient and modern contexts.

Female Figures in the Myth

Female figures in the myth of Hercules play a crucial role in shaping the narrative and influencing the hero's journey. While Hercules is often depicted as the quintessential male hero, the women in his story embody various archetypes that reflect the complexities of both divine and mortal femininity. From powerful goddesses to tragic figures, these women contribute to the themes of strength, sacrifice, and transformation. Their presence not only enriches the storyline but also serves as a counterpoint to Hercules' character, highlighting the multifaceted nature of heroism.

One of the most significant female figures is Hera, the queen of the gods. Her relationship with Hercules is fraught with tension, as she sees him as a constant reminder of her husband Zeus's infidelity. Hera's jealousy leads her to instigate numerous challenges for Hercules, including the madness that drives him to kill his own family. This act of violence sets the stage for his Twelve Labors, illustrating how the actions of a powerful woman can profoundly impact a hero's destiny. Hera's influence reflects the theme of adversity in the myth, suggesting that the struggles Hercules faces are not solely external but also a result of divine wrath.

Another important female figure is Atalanta, a skilled huntress who represents independence and strength. In the myth of the Calydonian Boar, she is the one who first injures the beast, showcasing her prowess in a male-dominated world. Atalanta's role serves as a reminder that women can be equally formidable as their male counterparts. Her presence in Hercules' narrative reinforces the idea that heroism is not limited to traditional masculine traits but can also encompass qualities such as cunning, bravery, and resilience. Atalanta's character invites readers to consider the diverse ways women can embody strength and challenge societal norms.

The figure of Deianira, Hercules' wife, introduces themes of love, loyalty, and sacrifice. Her tragic fate, driven by jealousy and manipulation, leads to Hercules' demise. Deianira's story underscores the complexities of female agency and the consequences of emotional turmoil. It raises questions about the often-painful intersections of love and power, illustrating how even well-intentioned actions can lead to disastrous outcomes. Through Deianira, the myth explores the darker aspects of femininity, emphasizing that women, too, can be caught in a web of fate that shapes their lives and the lives of those around them.

The female figures in the myth of Hercules collectively challenge the notion of a singular heroic narrative. They showcase the varied dimensions of womanhood, from nurturing and supportive roles to those that embody vengeance and tragedy. By analyzing these characters, readers can gain insight into the cultural values of ancient Greece and how they reflected gender dynamics. The inclusion of powerful women in Hercules' journey not only enhances the story but also invites contemporary audiences to re-evaluate the roles of women in mythology and their relevance in today's society.

Modern Feminist Interpretations

Modern feminist interpretations of the Twelve Labors of Hercules provide a fresh lens through which to analyze the roles of women within these ancient narratives. Traditionally, the stories surrounding Hercules have been dominated by male perspectives, often overshadowing the contributions and significance of female characters. Feminist scholars emphasize the necessity of recognizing these women not merely as supporting figures, but as integral components of the narrative that challenge the hero's journey and offer critical commentary on gender roles in ancient society.

One prominent interpretation highlights the figures of Hera and Megara, both of whom represent complex female archetypes. Hera, as the goddess of marriage and family, embodies the theme of jealousy and retribution, showcasing the consequences of Hercules' actions and his failure to honor divine relationships. Megara, Hercules' first wife, serves as a tragic figure whose life is irrevocably altered by Hercules' madness, stemming from Hera's influence. These characters illustrate how women's experiences are intertwined with the hero's narrative and how their suffering reflects the societal expectations imposed on women during that era.

Moreover, feminist readings of Hercules' labors reveal deeper insights into the nature of strength and heroism. The labors themselves are often seen as a series of trials that test Hercules' physical prowess, yet they also expose the vulnerabilities and challenges faced by women. By analyzing the tasks Hercules undertakes, such as slaying the Nemean Lion or capturing the Golden Hind, we can draw parallels to the struggles women endure in patriarchal societies, where their worth is frequently measured by their ability to endure and overcome adversity.

This perspective allows for a reimagining of heroism that encompasses both male and female experiences.

Additionally, modern feminist interpretations advocate for the inclusion of women's voices and experiences within the mythological framework. By exploring how female characters influence Hercules' journey, scholars argue that these narratives can be recontextualized to highlight themes of resilience, agency, and empowerment. This shift in focus not only enriches our understanding of the original myths but also paves the way for contemporary representations of women in literature and media, encouraging a diverse array of stories that celebrate female strength and complexity.

In conclusion, the exploration of modern feminist interpretations of the Twelve Labors of Hercules sheds light on the often overlooked roles of women in these ancient myths. By examining the intricacies of female characters and their impact on the hero's journey, we gain a more nuanced understanding of the narratives that have shaped cultural perceptions of gender and strength. These interpretations challenge us to rethink traditional narratives and recognize the significance of women's experiences in both historical and contemporary contexts.

Chapter 5: Historical Context of the Hercules Myth

Ancient Greece and Its Cultural Landscape

Ancient Greece was a vibrant picture of cultural, philosophical, and artistic expression that laid the groundwork for many aspects of Western civilization. Its city-states, notably Athens and Sparta, were centers of political innovation, military prowess, and intellectual exploration. The rich mythology of ancient Greece, populated by gods, heroes, and mythical creatures, served not only as entertainment but also as a means to understand the human experience. Among these figures, Hercules stands out as a quintessential hero whose Twelve Labors symbolize the struggle against insurmountable odds, reflecting the values and challenges of the society that created him.

The Twelve Labors of Hercules emerged from a complex cultural landscape where myth and reality intertwined. Each labor represents a unique challenge that Hercules must face, often embodying various aspects of human struggle and resilience. These tasks were not merely physical feats; they also symbolized moral and ethical dilemmas that resonated with the ancient Greek worldview. The stories surrounding Hercules and his labors were often used to convey lessons about courage, perseverance, and the consequences of hubris, reinforcing societal norms and expectations.

In examining Hercules' labors through the lens of comparative mythology, parallels can be drawn with other heroic figures across different cultures. For example, the trials of Hercules can be likened to the journeys of figures such as Gilgamesh in Mesopotamian myths or the labors of the Hindu god Krishna. These heroes often face trials that test their strength, intellect, and moral fiber, highlighting universal themes of transformation and personal growth. By studying these narratives, one gains insight into the shared human experience and the archetypes that resonate across civilizations.

The role of women in the myths surrounding Hercules also warrants examination, particularly from a feminist perspective. Characters such as Hera, who plays a crucial part in Hercules' life as both an adversary and a catalyst for his challenges, illustrate the complex dynamics of gender within these stories. While Hercules is often positioned as the central hero, the women in his myths contribute significantly to the narrative, shaping his path and influencing his actions. This interplay invites a deeper analysis of gender roles and the portrayal of women within the broader context of ancient Greek society.

Ultimately, the legacy of Hercules and his Twelve Labors extends far beyond ancient Greece. His influence permeates modern culture, serving as a symbol of strength and a model for overcoming adversity. From literature to film, Hercules' story continues to inspire contemporary narratives about resilience and moral fortitude. As we decode the symbolism within his labors, it becomes clear that these ancient myths offer timeless insights into human nature, the struggle for self-discovery, and the values that shape our ethics and beliefs today.

The Evolution of Hercules' Character

The character of Hercules has undergone significant evolution throughout history, reflecting changes in cultural values, societal norms, and psychological understandings. Initially depicted as a demigod with immense physical strength, Hercules was celebrated for his heroic feats and valor. However, as the myth evolved, so too did his character, transforming from a simplistic figure of brute strength to a more complex representation of the human experience. This shift is evident in the way Hercules' labors are interpreted, where the emphasis transitions from mere physical accomplishments to profound personal challenges that resonate with the struggles of everyday life.

In ancient Greek mythology, Hercules was often portrayed as a tragic hero, burdened by the weight of his own identity and the expectations placed upon him. The Twelve Labors, assigned to him as a form of penance, serve as a narrative device that not only showcases his physical prowess but also reflects his inner turmoil and journey toward redemption. Each labor, whether it involves slaying the Nemean Lion or capturing the Golden Hind, symbolizes deeper psychological battles that Hercules must confront, aligning him with the archetypal hero who faces adversity and emerges transformed.

As the myth of Hercules spread across cultures, his character began to embody various archetypes relevant to the societies interpreting his story. In Roman adaptations, for example, Hercules became a symbol of virtue and moral strength, often associated with the ideals of citizenship and duty. This transformation highlights the adaptability of the Hercules myth, as different cultures infused their own values and beliefs into his character. The evolution of Hercules, therefore, serves as a mirror reflecting the shifting ideals of heroism, from physical strength to moral integrity and psychological resilience.

The role of women in Hercules' story also illustrates the evolution of his character and the surrounding narratives. While the original myths often sidelined female figures, contemporary interpretations have sought to highlight their significance, portraying characters such as Deianira and Megara as integral to Hercules' journey. This shift not only enriches the narrative but also offers a feminist perspective, emphasizing the importance of collaborative strength and the impact of relationships on personal growth. The evolving portrayal of these female characters allows for a more nuanced understanding of Hercules as both a hero and a flawed individual navigating complex dynamics.

In modern pop culture, Hercules continues to evolve, reflecting contemporary values and ethics through various interpretations in film, literature, and art. These adaptations often emphasize themes of resilience, teamwork, and emotional intelligence, shifting the focus from sheer physicality to the importance of mental and emotional strength. The character of Hercules thus remains relevant, illustrating how timeless myths can adapt to resonate with new generations. This evolution not only preserves the legacy of Hercules but also invites ongoing dialogue about heroism, personal growth, and the symbolic significance of overcoming adversity in a rapidly changing world.

Influence of Historical Events on the Myth

The myth of Hercules and his Twelve Labors is deeply intertwined with the historical events and cultural shifts of ancient Greece. Hercules, a half-god and half-mortal, embodies the values and challenges faced by the society that created him. His exploits were not merely tales of heroism but reflections of the struggles and aspirations of the Greek people during significant periods of their history. From the rise of city-states to the influence of warfare, these historical contexts shaped the narrative and characteristics of Hercules, making him a symbol of strength and resilience against adversity.

In the backdrop of the myth, the historical context of the Greek Dark Ages and the subsequent Archaic and Classical periods played a crucial role in shaping the figure of Hercules. During these times, Greece experienced significant social and political changes that influenced the themes within the myth. The transition from tribal societies to more organized city-states brought about new challenges. Hercules' labors can be viewed as a metaphor for the collective struggle of the Greek people as they sought to define their identity and overcome the adversities of their time, including invasions and internal conflicts.

The Twelve Labors themselves reflect not only personal trials but also historical realities. For instance, the Nemean Lion, which Hercules must defeat, symbolizes the ferocity of the beasts that roamed the land as well as the overwhelming challenges faced by communities. Similarly, the capture of the Golden Hind and the cleaning of the Augean stables can be seen as allegories for the need to establish order and cleanliness in a society that was often chaotic and disordered. Each labor serves as a reminder of the historical struggles that required both physical strength and strategic thinking, mirroring the attributes valued by ancient Greek society.

Moreover, the role of divine intervention in Hercules' journey highlights the complex relationship between mortals and gods in ancient Greek culture. The gods often acted as both benefactors and obstacles, reflecting the unpredictability of fate and fortune in real life. Historical events that saw the rise and fall of various city-states and the capricious nature of war can be paralleled with the divine influences on Hercules. This dynamic not only enriched the myth but also provided a framework for understanding the significance of divine favor and the concept of heroism within the historical context of the time.

As the myth of Hercules evolved, it continued to be shaped by subsequent historical events, including the Hellenistic period and the Roman Empire's expansion. The adaptability of Hercules' narrative allowed it to resonate with different cultures and eras, highlighting universal themes of struggle, strength, and redemption. The historical influences on Hercules and his Twelve Labors ultimately serve as a testament to the enduring power of mythology as a means of interpreting human experience, reflecting the values and challenges of societies throughout history.

Chapter 6: Symbolism in the Twelve Labors

The Meaning Behind Each Labor

The Twelve Labors of Hercules serve as more than just a series of feats; each labor encapsulates a deeper meaning that resonates with various aspects of human experience. These tasks represent not only physical challenges but also psychological and moral trials that mirror the struggles individuals face in their own lives. Each labor can be interpreted through different lenses, offering insights into themes such as perseverance, redemption, and the quest for identity, making them relevant across cultures and generations.

The first labor, the Nemean Lion, symbolizes the confrontation with inner demons. Hercules must confront a beast that appears invincible, mirroring the struggles people face when dealing with their own fears and self-doubt. By defeating the lion, Hercules demonstrates the importance of courage and resilience in overcoming obstacles that seem insurmountable. This labor teaches that true strength comes not just from physical prowess but from the ability to face one's fears head-on.

In contrast, the second labor, the Lernaean Hydra, introduces the concept of growth through adversity. As Hercules battles the multi-headed serpent, each severed head gives rise to two more, symbolizing the cyclical nature of challenges in life. This labor illustrates the idea that setbacks can lead to increased difficulties, yet also encourages the pursuit of knowledge and strategy in overcoming them. The Hydra serves as a reminder that progress often requires persistence and the willingness to adapt, reinforcing that growth can emerge from difficult experiences.

The role of women in Hercules' labors is also significant, particularly in the labor involving the Ceryneian Hind. This labor signifies the importance of respect and understanding for the feminine aspects of nature and life. The hind, a sacred creature, represents the need for harmony with the world around us. Hercules' quest to capture it without harming it highlights themes of compassion and reverence for life, suggesting that true strength lies in the ability to coexist peacefully with others, including those who embody traditionally feminine qualities of grace and gentleness.

Another labor, the Erymanthian Boar, reflects the struggle for balance between chaos and order. Capturing the boar represents the integration of wild instincts into civilized behavior, emphasizing the importance of control over one's impulses. This labor serves as a metaphor for the human experience, where individuals must learn to manage their inner chaos to achieve personal harmony. Hercules' success in this labor is a testament to the power of discipline and the necessity of facing and taming the more primal aspects of ourselves.

Ultimately, the Twelve Labors of Hercules encapsulate meanings that extend far beyond ancient mythology. Each labor serves as a metaphor for personal growth, resilience, and the complexities of human existence. By examining these labors through various perspectives, we gain a deeper appreciation of Hercules not only as a mythological hero but as a symbol of the universal struggles we all face in our journey toward self-discovery and empowerment.

Representations of Strength and Weakness

In the myth of Hercules, representations of strength and weakness are intricately woven into the fabric of each of his twelve labors. Strength is often depicted through Hercules' physical prowess, his ability to confront and defeat formidable beasts, and his capacity to perform seemingly impossible tasks. For instance, when he slays the Nemean Lion, he not only showcases immense physical strength but also strategic thinking, as he must find a way to defeat a creature with impenetrable skin. This labor symbolizes the triumph of brute force, underscoring the cultural value placed on physical strength in ancient Greek society. However, each labor also reveals the nuances of weakness, often manifesting as vulnerability, emotional turmoil, or the consequences of hubris.

The concept of weakness is particularly significant in the context of Hercules' character development. Hercules, despite his extraordinary abilities, is not immune to failings. His struggles with madness, instigated by the goddess Hera, lead him to commit acts that he later regrets, highlighting the psychological dimensions of his character. This portrayal invites a deeper understanding of human frailty and the internal battles that accompany personal strength. It suggests that true heroism is not merely about physical domination but also about grappling with one's inner demons and seeking redemption.

Feminist perspectives on the labors reveal another layer of representation regarding strength and weakness. Many of the female figures in Hercules' narratives, such as Hera and Deianira, wield significant power that can both empower and constrain Hercules. Hera's relentless pursuit of Hercules reflects the complexities of female strength, as she embodies both vengeful power and protective instincts. Deianira's tragic mistake with the poisoned shirt represents the consequences of weakness, illustrating how vulnerability can lead to devastating outcomes. Through these portrayals, the myth critiques traditional notions of masculinity and invites discussions on the strength inherent in femininity.

The symbolic nature of Hercules' labors also speaks to broader themes of overcoming adversity, a concept that resonates across various cultures and mythologies. Each labor serves as an allegory for challenges that individuals face in their own lives, highlighting the spectrum of strength and weakness that can manifest during struggles. The ability to confront fears, endure hardships, and ultimately rise above them is a universal theme that transcends the myth itself. This duality reflects the human experience, where moments of weakness can lead to personal growth and a deeper understanding of one's capabilities.

In contemporary society, Hercules remains a symbol of strength, but the interpretation of this strength has evolved. Modern adaptations often depict him as a more nuanced character, one who embodies not only physical might but also emotional depth and vulnerability. This shift acknowledges that true strength involves a balance of both power and humility, challenging the rigid dichotomy of strength versus weakness. As a cultural icon, Hercules continues to inspire discussions about the complexities of human experience, urging individuals to embrace their strengths while recognizing and learning from their weaknesses.

The Labors as Metaphors for Life Challenges

The Twelve Labors of Hercules serve as powerful metaphors that encapsulate the myriad challenges individuals face throughout their lives. Each labor represents a distinct struggle, illustrating the idea that life is filled with obstacles that require perseverance, courage, and ingenuity to overcome. From the slaying of the Nemean Lion to the capturing of the Golden Hind, these tasks resonate with universal themes of conflict and resolution, encouraging individuals to confront and navigate their own hardships. The symbolic nature of these labors invites readers to reflect on their personal experiences and the broader human condition, highlighting the importance of resilience in the face of adversity.

In the context of comparative mythology, Hercules' labors parallel the trials encountered by heroes from various cultures, reinforcing the idea that the journey of overcoming challenges is a shared human experience. For instance, the epic quests of figures like Gilgamesh or Odysseus echo similar motifs of struggle and triumph. These narratives often center around the hero's growth, emphasizing that challenges are not just obstacles but opportunities for personal development. By examining Hercules' labors alongside those of other mythological heroes, readers can appreciate the common archetypes that emerge across cultures, illustrating how these stories have shaped our understanding of heroism and resilience.

Psychologically, Hercules embodies the archetype of the hero, representing the inner battles individuals face as they strive for personal growth. Each labor can be seen as a manifestation of internal conflicts, such as fear, doubt, and temptation. By confronting these challenges, Hercules not only seeks redemption but also undergoes profound transformation. This journey resonates with the psychological concept of individuation, where the integration of various aspects of the self leads to a more complete identity. Readers can find inspiration in Hercules' ability to confront his flaws and emerge stronger, serving as a reminder that personal struggles are integral to self-discovery and development.

Feminist perspectives on the labors reveal the significant roles women play in Hercules' journey, often serving as catalysts for his actions or embodying the challenges he must overcome. Figures such as Megara and Deianira illustrate the complexities of female agency within the narrative, challenging traditional gender roles. By analyzing these characters, readers are encouraged to consider the implications of gender dynamics in the context of struggle and support. This examination highlights the interplay between male and female experiences, emphasizing that the path to overcoming adversity is not solely a solitary endeavor but often involves collaboration and understanding among individuals of diverse backgrounds.

Ultimately, the Twelve Labors of Hercules stand as a testament to the enduring nature of human struggle and resilience. They reflect the idea that challenges are not merely obstacles to be avoided but essential components of the human experience. By engaging with these stories, readers can draw parallels to their own lives, recognizing that, like Hercules, they too possess the strength to confront their labors. This symbolic journey encourages a deeper understanding of the values and ethics we cultivate through our struggles, leaving a lasting legacy that informs contemporary views on personal growth, community, and the human spirit.

Chapter 7: The Influence of Hercules on Modern Pop Culture

Hercules in Film and Television

Hercules has long been a captivating figure in film and television, serving as a bridge between ancient mythology and modern storytelling. His tales have been adapted in various forms, from animated features to live-action films and television series, each offering a unique interpretation of the legendary hero and his twelve labors. These adaptations not only entertain but also provide insight into how the character of Hercules has evolved to reflect contemporary values, challenges, and societal norms. The enduring popularity of Hercules in visual media showcases the timelessness of his narrative, as well as the universal themes of strength, perseverance, and redemption.

One of the most notable adaptations of Hercules is Disney's animated film released in 1997. This version presents a lighter, family-friendly take on the myth, infusing humor and music into the story. While it simplifies many aspects of the original myths, it introduces key themes such as the struggle for identity and the importance of personal choices. The film's portrayal of Hercules as an underdog resonates with audiences, particularly younger viewers, who see in him a relatable character navigating the challenges of growing up. The film also incorporates strong female characters, such as Megara, who challenge traditional gender roles and add depth to the narrative.

Television adaptations have further expanded the portrayal of Hercules, with shows like "Hercules: The Legendary Journeys" in the 1990s and its spin-off "Xena: Warrior Princess." These series delve deeper into the complexities of Hercules' character and his relationships with other mythological figures. They explore themes of friendship, loyalty, and moral dilemmas, often placing Hercules in situations where he must confront not only physical challenges but also ethical questions. This approach allows for a more nuanced exploration of his character, emphasizing the psychological aspects of heroism and the internal struggles that accompany his external labors.

The representation of women in these adaptations has sparked discussions about feminist perspectives in the context of Hercules' story. While the original myths often sidelined female characters, modern interpretations have sought to elevate their roles, showcasing strong, independent women who are not merely supporting characters but active participants in the narrative. By reimagining figures such as Hera, Athena, and even the women Hercules encounters during his labors, these adaptations highlight the importance of female agency and challenge the traditional patriarchal narratives found in ancient texts.

In addition to character representation, the symbolism inherent in Hercules' labors is often explored in film and television, providing viewers with a deeper understanding of what each task represents. From the Nemean Lion to the Golden Apples of the Hesperides, each labor serves as a metaphor for personal growth and the human condition. Through these stories, audiences can reflect on their own struggles and the means by which they confront adversity. The legacy of Hercules in film and television is not just about entertainment; it invites viewers to engage with the archetypal themes of heroism, resilience, and the quest for self-understanding in a rapidly changing world.

Adaptations and Reinterpretations

Adaptations and reinterpretations of the myth of Hercules and his Twelve Labors have emerged across various cultures and eras, each offering a unique perspective on the hero's journey. From ancient Greece to modern-day cinema, the story of Hercules resonates with audiences due to its universal themes of strength, perseverance, and moral challenges. These adaptations often reflect the values and concerns of the societies that produce them, showcasing how the myth continues to evolve while retaining its core elements.

In the realm of comparative mythology, Hercules serves as a template for understanding similar heroic figures across different cultures. For instance, the labors he undertakes parallel the quests of heroes in other mythologies, such as Gilgamesh in Mesopotamian lore or Beowulf in Anglo-Saxon tales. Each hero faces formidable challenges that test their character and resolve, illustrating a common archetype of the hero's journey. By examining these parallels, one can appreciate how the myth of Hercules not only stands alone but also contributes to a broader discourse on heroism and human struggle.

Psychological interpretations of Hercules emphasize the archetypal journey of self-discovery and personal growth. The Twelve Labors can be viewed as allegories for internal conflicts and the trials one must face in the process of maturation. Each labor represents a facet of the human experience, such as the battle against one's own fears or the quest for redemption. This psychological lens allows modern audiences to connect with Hercules on a personal level, making his journey relevant to contemporary discussions on mental health, resilience, and the pursuit of identity.

Feminist perspectives on Hercules' labors reveal the often-overlooked roles of women in the myth. While Hercules is celebrated for his strength and valor, the women he encounters—such as Megara, Deianira, and the various goddesses—play pivotal roles in shaping his narrative. These characters often embody the consequences of Hercules' actions and decisions, highlighting themes of agency, sacrifice, and the struggle for power. By reinterpreting these figures' stories, scholars and storytellers alike can challenge traditional narratives and bring attention to the complexities of gender dynamics within the myth.

The legacy of Hercules in modern pop culture underscores his enduring influence. Films, television series, and literature frequently draw upon the archetypes and themes present in the original myths, reimagining Hercules as a symbol of contemporary values. Whether depicted as a superhero or a flawed character grappling with his past, Hercules remains a figure through which audiences explore ideas of strength, morality, and the human condition. These adaptations not only ensure the survival of the myth but also invite new interpretations that resonate with changing societal norms and ethical considerations.

Hercules in Literature and Art

Hercules has captivated audiences across generations, not only through ancient texts but also through various forms of literature and art. The character's origins can be traced back to Greek mythology, where he was revered as a demigod known for his extraordinary strength and bravery. His Twelve Labors, which he undertook to atone for a grave mistake, serve as a rich narrative framework that has inspired countless adaptations. From epic poems like "The Iliad" and "The Odyssey" to modern novels and graphic novels, Hercules embodies the archetype of the hero facing insurmountable challenges, resonating with the universal themes of struggle, redemption, and heroism.

In visual art, Hercules has been a prominent figure since ancient times, appearing in sculptures, pottery, and frescoes. Artists have depicted him in various stages of his labors, emphasizing not just his physical prowess but also the emotional and psychological aspects of his journey. For instance, the depiction of Hercules battling the Nemean Lion often symbolizes the confrontation with one's own fears, while the capture of the Golden Hind reflects the pursuit of elusive goals. These artistic representations enhance the narrative of Hercules, inviting viewers to explore deeper meanings behind each labor and the transformative nature of his experiences.

Comparative mythology reveals that Hercules is not an isolated figure; his archetype can be found in numerous cultures around the world. Heroes like Gilgamesh, Beowulf, and even modern characters like Superman share traits with Hercules, showcasing the enduring nature of the heroic journey. These similarities highlight common human experiences of adversity and triumph, suggesting that the story of Hercules transcends cultural and temporal boundaries. By examining these parallels, readers can gain insights into the shared values and struggles that define humanity across different societies.

The psychological analysis of Hercules also presents an intriguing perspective on his character. He embodies the classic hero's journey, marked by trials that lead to personal growth and self-discovery. Each labor can be viewed as a metaphor for the challenges individuals face in their own lives, making Hercules a relatable figure for those navigating their personal struggles. Furthermore, the divine intervention that helps Hercules in his endeavors raises questions about the balance between fate and free will, inviting readers to reflect on their own life paths and the forces that shape their outcomes.

Feminist perspectives on the Hercules myth reveal the often-overlooked roles of female characters in his labors. Figures such as Hera, who plays a significant role in Hercules' trials, and the various women he encounters, contribute to the narrative in ways that challenge traditional gender roles. By analyzing these characters, readers can uncover layers of meaning that reflect societal attitudes toward women and their power. This exploration enriches the understanding of Hercules' story, illustrating that while he may be the central figure, the contributions and complexities of female characters are integral to the myth's enduring legacy.

Chapter 8: The Labors of Hercules: A Study in Overcoming Adversity

Themes of Perseverance and Resilience

The themes of perseverance and resilience are central to the narrative of Hercules and his Twelve Labors, illustrating how the hero's journey reflects the challenges faced by individuals in their own lives. Each labor presents Herculean tasks that not only test his physical strength but also his mental endurance and determination. This duality serves as a powerful reminder that personal growth often arises from overcoming formidable obstacles, encouraging readers to embrace their own struggles as opportunities for development.

In mythological contexts, perseverance is often depicted through the relationship between a hero and their adversities. Hercules embodies this quality as he confronts seemingly insurmountable challenges, such as slaying the Nemean Lion and capturing the Golden Hind. These encounters symbolize the trials that everyone faces, reinforcing the idea that setbacks are a natural part of any journey. By witnessing Hercules' unyielding spirit, readers can draw parallels to their own experiences, understanding that resilience is fostered through perseverance in the face of adversity.

Resilience is further emphasized through the support of allies and the influence of divine intervention. While Hercules is known for his exceptional strength, the assistance from characters such as Athena and Hermes highlights the importance of community and collaboration. This aspect of the narrative teaches that resilience is not solely an individual trait; rather, it can be bolstered by the encouragement and support of others. In a modern context, this can be reflected in the importance of friendships, mentorships, and familial bonds during challenging times.

The psychological implications of Hercules' journey also shed light on internal struggles that resonate with many individuals. Each labor represents not only a physical challenge but also an emotional or psychological hurdle that Hercules must overcome. This layered interpretation allows readers to explore their own fears and insecurities, understanding that resilience is a multifaceted process. Engaging with these themes can inspire personal reflection and growth, as individuals recognize that they, too, possess the strength to navigate their own labors.

Ultimately, the enduring legacy of Hercules and his Twelve Labors serves as a testament to the human capacity for perseverance and resilience. By examining how these themes manifest in the myth, readers are encouraged to seek out their own sources of strength and motivation. The story of Hercules is not merely a tale of heroism; it is a call to action, urging individuals to recognize their potential to rise above challenges and to cultivate resilience in the face of life's inevitable struggles.

Lessons in Overcoming Obstacles

In exploring the lessons embedded within Hercules' trials, we uncover profound insights into overcoming obstacles that resonate across cultures and ages. Each of Hercules' Twelve Labors serves as a narrative framework that illustrates the struggles between human limitations and the pursuit of greatness. These stories not only highlight the physical challenges he faced but also represent deeper psychological and emotional hurdles. The myth encourages readers to confront their own adversities, suggesting that triumph often requires perseverance, ingenuity, and resilience.

Hercules' encounter with the Nemean Lion exemplifies the necessity of adapting one's approach in the face of insurmountable odds. Initially, Hercules attempts to defeat the lion using conventional weapons, only to realize that brute force is ineffective against such a formidable foe.

This moment of realization teaches an essential lesson: sometimes, to overcome obstacles, we must think creatively and employ unconventional strategies. The success of Hercules in strangling the lion with his bare hands symbolizes the importance of flexibility in problem-solving and the courage to reconsider one's methods when faced with failure.

Another significant labor, the capture of the Erymanthian Boar, illustrates the notion of patience and preparation. Hercules is tasked with capturing a beast that is both powerful and elusive. This labor underscores that overcoming obstacles is not merely about strength but also about the ability to plan and execute a strategy over time. Hercules' success in capturing the boar highlights the importance of persistence and the understanding that some challenges require thorough planning and a measured approach rather than hasty action. This theme resonates with individuals facing long-term challenges, reinforcing the idea that consistent effort can lead to eventual success.

Furthermore, Hercules' interactions with various figures throughout his labors, including the assistance of others and divine intervention, provide insight into the value of collaboration and seeking help when necessary. Many of Hercules' victories are not solely attributed to his strength but also to the support he receives from gods and allies. This aspect of the myth emphasizes that overcoming obstacles is often a communal effort, reminding us that seeking guidance and support from others can enhance our ability to navigate difficulties. It challenges the individualistic notion of heroism, suggesting that vulnerability and reliance on others are not weaknesses but rather strengths in the journey toward overcoming adversity.

Ultimately, the narrative of Hercules serves as a powerful metaphor for the human experience. The lessons learned from his labors encourage individuals to embrace challenges as opportunities for growth. By facing obstacles with creativity, patience, collaboration, and resilience, one can emerge stronger and more capable. Hercules' journey illustrates that the path to overcoming adversity is multifaceted, and the wisdom derived from these mythic struggles continues to inspire personal development and cultural values today. The enduring legacy of Hercules reminds us that while obstacles are inevitable, how we respond to them defines our character and ultimately shapes our destiny.

Hercules as a Model for Personal Challenges

Hercules, the legendary hero of ancient Greek mythology, serves as an enduring symbol of personal challenges and triumph over adversity. His Twelve Labors, a series of seemingly insurmountable tasks imposed upon him, reflect the struggles that individuals often face in their own lives. Each labor represents a distinct challenge that Hercules must confront, not only showcasing his physical strength but also his resilience, intelligence, and moral fortitude. These traits resonate with audiences, particularly those aged twelve and up, who may be navigating their own personal challenges and seeking inspiration in the face of adversity.

The first labor, the Nemean Lion, highlights the importance of confronting fears. Hercules learns that brute strength alone is not enough; he must adapt his approach and think creatively to overcome the lion's impenetrable hide. This labor teaches a crucial lesson about the necessity of strategy and perseverance. In life, challenges often seem daunting, but like Hercules, individuals can find innovative ways to tackle obstacles. This labor encourages young readers to embrace their fears and view them as opportunities for growth rather than insurmountable barriers.

In contrast, the second labor, the Lernaean Hydra, emphasizes the idea of overcoming multiple issues at once. Each time Hercules cuts off one head of the Hydra, two more grow back. This symbolizes the complexity of personal challenges, where solving one problem can lead to the emergence of others. The lesson here is that persistence is key; Hercules ultimately learns to cauterize the necks to prevent the heads from regenerating. For young people, this labor serves as a reminder that challenges often require sustained effort and adaptability. The ability to stay focused and find new solutions in the face of overwhelming odds is a vital skill that can be applied in various aspects of life.

The journey through the Twelve Labors also reveals the importance of seeking help and recognizing the value of collaboration. Hercules frequently receives assistance from allies, such as Athena and Iolaus. This aspect of the myth underscores that while personal challenges can feel isolating, support from friends, family, or mentors can be invaluable. Young individuals are encouraged to foster relationships and seek guidance when facing their own trials, reinforcing the idea that asking for help is a sign of strength rather than weakness.

Finally, Hercules' ultimate success in completing the Twelve Labors demonstrates the transformative power of resilience and determination. His journey from a state of despair, having been driven mad and committing acts he could not control, to becoming a celebrated hero serves as a powerful narrative of redemption. For readers, this arc can inspire a sense of hope; it illustrates that personal challenges, no matter how severe, can lead to growth and new opportunities. Hercules embodies the idea that through hard work, self-reflection, and courage, anyone can emerge victorious from their struggles, ultimately shaping their identity and values in the process.

Chapter 9: The Role of Divine Intervention in Hercules' Success

The Gods and Their Influence

The influence of the gods in the myth of Hercules is profound and multifaceted, shaping not only his character but also the trajectory of his legendary Twelve Labors. In ancient Greek mythology, gods and goddesses serve as powerful forces that dictate the fates of mortals. Hercules, born of divine lineage as the son of Zeus, embodies the complexities of this relationship. His labors are not merely tests of strength and skill; they are also reflections of the will and whims of the gods, who intervene in both benevolent and malevolent ways throughout his journey.

One of the most significant aspects of divine influence is the role of Hera, the wife of Zeus and the principal antagonist in Hercules' life. Her jealousy of Hercules, stemming from his illegitimate birth, manifests in numerous trials that he must overcome. This conflict is emblematic of the struggle between mortal agency and divine interference, highlighting how the gods can complicate a hero's path. Hera's relentless pursuit of Hercules through various challenges serves as a reminder that even the mightiest heroes are not immune to the struggles imposed by higher powers.

In contrast, other deities, such as Athena and Hermes, play supportive roles in Hercules' adventures. Athena often provides wisdom and guidance, while Hermes assists in his quests with speed and cunning. This duality of divine influence illustrates a key theme in mythology: the necessity of both struggle and support in the journey toward personal growth. Hercules' ability to navigate these relationships with the divine reflects the psychological archetypes of heroism, where the hero must confront not only external challenges but also internal conflicts shaped by their connections to the gods.

The Twelve Labors themselves are rich in symbolism, often representing various human struggles and virtues. Each labor can be viewed as a metaphor for personal challenges, such as the need to confront and overcome fear, anger, or despair. The divine influence on these labors serves to elevate them beyond mere physical challenges; they become allegories for the moral and ethical dilemmas faced by individuals. By understanding the gods' roles, one can appreciate how these mythic narratives resonate with contemporary values, encouraging individuals to reflect on their personal journeys and the forces that shape them.

Ultimately, the gods' influence in the story of Hercules transcends the realm of myth, offering insights into the human experience. The interplay between divine intervention and human agency raises essential questions about fate, free will, and the nature of strength. As modern audiences engage with the Hercules myth, they discover not only a tale of heroism but also a tale of cultural interpretations that continue to inform our understanding of resilience, adversity, and the enduring impact of myth on contemporary life.

Fate vs. Free Will in Hercules' Journey

In the journey of Hercules, the tension between fate and free will plays a crucial role in shaping his character and experiences. Hercules, born as a demigod, was subject to the whims of both the gods and his own choices. His trials, known as the Twelve Labors, serve as a reflection of this conflict. While the gods often intervene in his life, it is Hercules' responses to these challenges that highlight the importance of personal agency. This duality raises questions about how much of his journey is predetermined and how much is a product of his own decisions.

Fate, as portrayed in Greek mythology, often manifests through prophecies and divine decrees. For Hercules, his fate is heavily influenced by the jealousy of Hera, who seeks to undermine him from the moment of his birth. This antagonism sets the stage for his trials, suggesting that his path is fraught with difficulties laid out by forces beyond his control. However, Hercules' strength and determination allow him to confront these challenges head-on, revealing that while fate may chart a course, it does not dictate the choices he makes along the way.

The concept of free will is vividly illustrated in Hercules' approach to each labor. Each task, from slaying the Nemean Lion to capturing the Golden Hind, requires not only physical strength but also cleverness and moral choices. Hercules must navigate his own desires, fears, and instincts to succeed. His ability to choose how to respond to the challenges presented to him emphasizes the significance of his agency, highlighting that even when faced with daunting fate, one has the power to shape their destiny through action and resolve.

Moreover, the interplay of fate and free will is further complicated by the role of divine intervention. The gods frequently assist or hinder Hercules, suggesting that while he has the power to choose, those choices are often influenced by the will of higher powers. This relationship raises deeper philosophical questions about the nature of heroism. Is Hercules truly a hero because of his choices, or are his accomplishments merely a result of divine favor? This ambiguity invites readers to consider how much of their own lives are guided by external forces versus their individual decisions.

Ultimately, Hercules' journey serves as a profound metaphor for the human experience. The struggle between fate and free will is universal, resonating with anyone who grapples with the complexities of their own life circumstances. Through Hercules, we learn that while fate may set the stage, it is our choices that define our character and legacy. This realization encourages a deeper understanding of personal responsibility, inviting individuals to embrace their agency in the face of adversity, much like the legendary hero himself.

Key Moments of Divine Assistance

In the tale of Hercules and his Twelve Labors, moments of divine assistance play a crucial role in shaping the hero's journey. These interventions often come from the gods, highlighting a recurring theme in mythology: the interplay between human effort and divine favor. One notable example is when Athena, the goddess of wisdom, provides guidance and support to Hercules as he confronts daunting challenges. Her presence symbolizes the importance of strategic thinking and intelligence in overcoming obstacles, suggesting that brute strength alone is insufficient for success.

Another significant moment occurs during Hercules' encounter with the Nemean Lion. Initially, he struggles to defeat this seemingly invincible beast. It is with the divine assistance of Zeus that he gains the insight to use the lion's own strength against it. This moment underscores the belief that divine intervention often manifests as inspiration or sudden clarity, allowing Hercules to tap into deeper resources within himself. The lesson here emphasizes that heroes are not just defined by their physical prowess but also by their ability to innovate and adapt.

The role of Hera in Hercules' life further illustrates the complexity of divine assistance. As Hercules' stepmother, Hera often acts as an antagonist, setting challenges before him. However, her actions inadvertently lead to moments of growth and transformation. This dynamic suggests that adversities, even those instigated by divine forces, can serve as catalysts for personal development. Hercules' ability to rise above Hera's trials reflects a fundamental theme in mythology: the idea that struggle is an integral part of the hero's path toward self-discovery and actualization.

Moreover, the divine assistance of Hermes is evident during Hercules' quest for the golden apples of the Hesperides. Hermes not only provides guidance but also serves as a messenger, linking Hercules to the divine realm. This relationship illustrates the interconnectedness of the mortal and divine worlds, emphasizing that heroes often require support beyond their immediate capabilities. The act of seeking help from the gods reinforces the idea that collaboration and community—whether with fellow humans or divine beings—are essential for overcoming life's challenges.

Ultimately, these key moments of divine assistance highlight the multifaceted nature of Hercules' journey. They reveal how divine forces shape the narrative of struggle and triumph, suggesting that the path to greatness is seldom a solitary endeavor. The interactions between Hercules and the gods serve as a reminder that while personal strength and determination are vital, the influence of divine support can provide the necessary boost to achieve the extraordinary. This theme resonates across various cultural interpretations of heroism, reinforcing the idea that even the mightiest heroes rely on the unseen forces that guide them toward their destiny.

Chapter 10: Hercules as a Symbol of Strength

Cultural Interpretations of Strength

The concept of strength in the context of Hercules and his Twelve Labors can be interpreted in various cultural frameworks, each adding depth to our understanding of this iconic hero. In ancient Greece, physical prowess was paramount, embodied in Hercules' feats against formidable foes like the Nemean Lion and the Hydra. His strength was not merely a matter of brawn; it represented a moral and ethical dimension, underscoring the belief that true strength involves courage and integrity in the face of overwhelming challenges. This cultural lens emphasizes that Hercules' physical abilities were a means to an end, serving higher values that resonated with the societal ideals of heroism.

As we explore other mythologies, the interpretation of strength takes on different meanings. For example, in Norse mythology, strength is often coupled with wisdom, as seen in figures like Thor, who represents a balance of might and intellect. This contrasts with Hercules, whose strength is sometimes depicted as both a blessing and a curse, leading to moments of vulnerability. Cultures such as those in India also present heroes like Hanuman, where strength is linked to devotion and spiritual power. This comparative perspective highlights that while physical strength is a common theme, its implications and associations vary significantly across different cultural narratives.

In contemporary discussions, psychological interpretations of Hercules' strength focus on personal growth and overcoming internal struggles. The Twelve Labors serve as metaphors for the trials individuals face in their own lives, reflecting the idea that true strength is often found in resilience and self-discovery. This approach aligns with modern psychological frameworks that emphasize emotional intelligence and the importance of mental fortitude. Hercules' journey becomes a symbol for anyone grappling with their own challenges, reinforcing the notion that strength is not solely about physical capabilities but also involves emotional and psychological endurance.

Feminist perspectives provide another important cultural interpretation of strength within the Hercules myth. Women in the labors, such as the Amazonian warriors or the goddess Athena, illustrate that strength is not limited to male characters. These women often play crucial roles in guiding or challenging Hercules, highlighting the necessity of collaboration between genders. This interpretation challenges traditional notions of heroism, suggesting that the strength displayed by female characters is equally essential and deserves recognition. By examining these roles, we can appreciate that strength manifests in many forms, including wisdom, support, and resilience.

Lastly, the influence of Hercules on modern pop culture reflects ongoing interpretations of strength. From films to graphic novels, representations of Hercules continue to evolve, often emphasizing themes of self-acceptance and the complexities of heroism. This contemporary portrayal invites audiences to reconsider what it means to be strong in today's society, suggesting that vulnerability can coexist with power. As cultures redefine strength in light of modern values, Hercules remains a poignant symbol, embodying the enduring struggle for personal and collective empowerment that resonates across time and space.

Hercules in Sports and Competitions

Hercules, often celebrated as the epitome of strength and bravery, has been a central figure in sports and competitions, both in ancient mythology and in modern interpretations. The twelve labors of Hercules are not merely tales of physical feats; they also symbolize the competitive spirit inherent in athletic pursuits. From his encounters with formidable beasts to his triumphs over daunting challenges, Hercules embodies the essence of competition, pushing boundaries and striving for excellence. This competitive nature resonates deeply with the values associated with sports, where perseverance, strength, and the will to overcome obstacles are paramount.

In ancient Greece, the significance of athletic competition was exemplified by the Olympic Games, which were established in honor of Zeus and included events that celebrated physical prowess. Hercules was often invoked as an emblem of strength and determination, inspiring athletes to achieve greatness. The connection between Hercules and sports can be seen in various myths where he competes against formidable opponents or engages in contests of skill. These stories not only showcase his physical capabilities but also highlight the moral and ethical dimensions of competition, such as honor, respect, and the importance of striving for one's personal best.

The competitive spirit of Hercules can also be analyzed through the lens of comparative mythology, where similar hero figures across cultures reflect universal themes of struggle and triumph. Just as Hercules faced numerous challenges, heroes in other mythologies engage in competitions that test their resolve and character. For example, the stories of Gilgamesh in Mesopotamian mythology and Beowulf in Anglo-Saxon lore illustrate the archetypal hero's journey, where overcoming adversities is central to their narratives. This commonality emphasizes how competition serves as a catalyst for growth and transformation, a theme that resonates with audiences across different cultures and eras.

From a psychological perspective, Hercules represents an archetype of the hero who must confront both external challenges and internal conflicts. His labors can be seen as a metaphor for personal struggles that individuals face in their own lives, particularly in the context of sports and competitions. Athletes often encounter obstacles that require not only physical strength but also mental resilience and emotional fortitude.

Hercules' journey encourages individuals to embrace their challenges, fostering personal growth and self-discovery through the competitive process. This psychological analysis enriches our understanding of how the figure of Hercules transcends mere myth, becoming a symbol of the human experience.

In contemporary culture, Hercules continues to influence sports and competition through various media representations, from films to video games, where his legendary feats inspire new generations. The legacy of Hercules as a figure of strength and competition serves as a motivational force, encouraging individuals to strive for excellence in their pursuits. As we decode the symbolic struggles inherent in the twelve labors, we can appreciate how Hercules not only embodies the spirit of competition but also reflects the enduring values of resilience, courage, and the relentless pursuit of one's goals. This connection between Hercules and sports ultimately reinforces the notion that the spirit of competition is a timeless and universal aspect of human nature.

Strength Beyond Physicality

The concept of strength in the myth of Hercules extends far beyond mere physical prowess. While Hercules is often celebrated for his incredible feats of strength, each of his Twelve Labors serves as a symbolic representation of the inner strength required to confront personal challenges and adversities. This dimension of strength encompasses resilience, courage, and the ability to confront one's fears, illustrating that true power often lies in mental and emotional fortitude rather than physical might.

In the context of comparative mythology, Hercules stands alongside other legendary heroes who embody similar themes of inner strength. Figures such as Theseus, Gilgamesh, and Perseus also face trials that test not only their physical capabilities but their moral character and resolve. Each hero's journey reflects a universal struggle—one that resonates with audiences across cultures and eras. The challenges they encounter often demand a blend of intellect, empathy, and strategic thinking, highlighting the multifaceted nature of strength in heroic narratives.

Psychologically, Hercules represents the archetype of the hero who must undergo transformation. His labors symbolize the trials individuals face in their own lives, serving as metaphors for personal growth and self-discovery. Each labor requires Hercules to confront different aspects of his psyche, from grappling with guilt and shame to embracing vulnerability and seeking redemption. This journey toward self-actualization illustrates that overcoming internal struggles can be as significant as defeating external foes, emphasizing that a hero's true strength is often found in their ability to evolve.

In examining the roles of women within the Hercules mythos, it becomes evident that strength is not solely embodied by male figures. The women in these narratives, such as Megara and Deianira, play crucial roles that highlight their own forms of resilience and agency. Their interactions with Hercules reveal the complexities of relationships and the importance of collaboration in overcoming adversities. This perspective challenges traditional notions of heroism, suggesting that both men and women possess unique strengths that contribute to the larger picture of heroic stories.

Finally, the legacy of Hercules in modern pop culture continues to reinforce the idea that strength transcends physicality. Contemporary representations often explore themes of vulnerability and emotional resilience, resonating with audiences who seek relatable heroes in an increasingly complex world. This evolution reflects society's growing recognition of diverse forms of strength, emphasizing that true heroism lies not just in conquering challenges but in the courage to face one's inner demons and the willingness to support others along their journeys.

Chapter 11: The Legacy of Hercules

Myths Shaping Contemporary Values

Myths have long been a powerful medium through which cultures convey their values, beliefs, and social norms. The story of Hercules and his Twelve Labors serves as a prime example of how ancient narratives continue to shape contemporary values. Each labor represents not only a physical challenge but also a moral and ethical framework that resonates with modern audiences. Themes such as perseverance, sacrifice, and the quest for identity are woven throughout Hercules' journeys, illustrating the timeless nature of these myths.

One prevalent myth surrounding Hercules is that of the "self-made hero." In a world often defined by individualism and personal achievement, Hercules embodies the struggle against insurmountable odds. His labors symbolize the journey of self-discovery and personal growth, encouraging contemporary individuals to confront their own challenges. This narrative promotes the idea that success is attainable through hard work and resilience, reinforcing a value system that prioritizes determination and tenacity in the face of adversity.

Moreover, the Twelve Labors of Hercules can be interpreted through a feminist lens, revealing the often-overlooked roles of women within the myth. Characters like Atalanta and Deianira provide critical commentary on gender dynamics and the expectations placed upon women. By examining these female figures, contemporary audiences can challenge traditional gender roles and appreciate the complexities of women's contributions to heroic narratives. This perspective encourages a more inclusive understanding of strength and heroism, broadening the values that emerge from Hercules' story.

The psychological dimensions of Hercules' journey also resonate with modern notions of archetypes and personal growth. Each labor can be viewed as a step in the hero's journey, illustrating various facets of human experience. From confronting one's fears to seeking redemption, these struggles mirror the psychological battles individuals face today. By engaging with Hercules' myth, contemporary audiences can reflect on their own lives, fostering a deeper understanding of resilience and the transformative power of confronting personal challenges.

Finally, the legacy of Hercules extends into popular culture, where his story continues to inspire films, literature, and other media. This ongoing relevance underscores the myth's ability to adapt and remain meaningful in contemporary society. The values embodied in Hercules' labors—strength, perseverance, and moral integrity—serve as guiding principles for modern audiences. As myths evolve, they retain their core messages, illustrating how ancient narratives can inform and shape the ethical frameworks and values of today's world.

Ethical Lessons from Hercules' Story

Hercules, the legendary hero of Greek mythology, embodies a range of ethical lessons that resonate through time, providing insights into human behavior, morality, and the complexities of life. His Twelve Labors are not merely tales of physical strength; they also serve as a framework for understanding challenges, responsibilities, and the moral choices that define character. Each labor presents Hercules not only with physical trials but also with ethical dilemmas that highlight the importance of courage, perseverance, and integrity in the face of adversity.

One significant lesson from Hercules' story is the value of responsibility. Tasked with completing the Twelve Labors as a form of penance, Hercules demonstrates that one must take ownership of their actions and face the consequences, regardless of the difficulty involved. This theme of accountability is critical, especially for young audiences who are beginning to navigate their own choices and the impact those choices have on themselves and others. Hercules' unwavering commitment to completing each labor serves as a reminder that true strength lies not just in physical prowess but in the willingness to confront one's past mistakes and strive for redemption.

Courage is another central ethical lesson illustrated through Hercules' journey. Each labor presents a formidable opponent or challenge—be it the Nemean Lion or the Hydra—representing not only external obstacles but also internal fears and doubts. Hercules' ability to confront these challenges head-on teaches the importance of bravery in personal growth. For the audience, particularly adolescents, this lesson can inspire the understanding that overcoming fear is a vital step toward achieving one's goals and that facing challenges is an essential part of the maturation process.

The role of compassion and empathy is also woven throughout Hercules' narrative, particularly in his interactions with others. While he is often seen as a figure of brute strength, his ability to help those in need—such as freeing Prometheus or aiding the distressed—highlights the ethical imperative to show kindness and support to others. This lesson encourages individuals to cultivate a sense of community and responsibility toward those who are vulnerable or in distress, reinforcing the idea that true heroism encompasses not only personal triumphs but also the welfare of others.

Lastly, the concept of humility emerges as a crucial ethical lesson from Hercules' story. Despite his immense strength and accomplishments, Hercules often experiences moments of vulnerability and doubt. These instances remind us that even the mightiest heroes can falter and that humility is essential in recognizing one's limitations. For young audiences, this lesson is vital in understanding that everyone, regardless of their achievements, should remain grounded and approachable. Hercules' journey encapsulates the idea that ethical growth involves recognizing our flaws and learning from them, fostering a more compassionate and understanding society.

Hercules in Modern Society and Education

Hercules, one of the most enduring figures from ancient mythology, continues to resonate in modern society and education. His Twelve Labors serve as a rich source of inspiration and analysis, offering insights into the human experience and the challenges we face. In contemporary classrooms, educators utilize Hercules' exploits to teach themes such as resilience, courage, and the importance of facing adversity. By examining these mythical tasks, students can engage in discussions about personal growth, character development, and the psychological archetypes represented by Hercules and his trials.

In comparative mythology, Hercules stands alongside similar heroes from various cultures, such as Gilgamesh, Beowulf, and Achilles. Each of these figures embodies unique qualities that reflect the values and beliefs of their respective societies. By studying these parallels, students gain a broader understanding of how different cultures interpret heroism and moral dilemmas. This comparative approach not only enriches their knowledge of mythology but also encourages critical thinking as they analyze the similarities and differences in these narratives.

The psychological analysis of Hercules reveals archetypal themes that are relevant to personal development. The struggles Hercules endures can be seen as metaphorical representations of the internal conflicts individuals face in their own lives. Themes of transformation, redemption, and the quest for identity are prevalent in his story, allowing students to explore their own journeys of self-discovery. By relating these ancient stories to modern psychological concepts, educators can help students understand the significance of overcoming personal challenges and the importance of resilience.

Feminist perspectives on Hercules shed light on the roles of women in his labors and the broader mythological narrative. Characters such as Megara, Deianira, and the various goddesses present in the myths challenge traditional gender roles and highlight the complexity of female figures in a predominantly male-driven story. Analyzing these characters allows for discussions about the representation of women in mythology and their impact on the hero's journey. This critical exploration encourages students to think about gender dynamics and the importance of inclusive narratives in both historical and contemporary contexts.

Lastly, the legacy of Hercules in modern pop culture and media illustrates his lasting influence on contemporary values and ethics. From films to literature, Hercules' character embodies the ideals of heroism, strength, and moral integrity that resonate with audiences today. By examining these modern representations, students can assess how ancient myths continue to shape societal norms and individual aspirations. Ultimately, the study of Hercules and his labors provides a multifaceted lens through which to understand not only the past but also the present and future of human experience.

Don't miss out!

Visit the website below and you can sign up to receive emails whenever Douglas Albert Amos publishes a new book. There's no charge and no obligation.

https://books2read.com/r/B-A-KPIWB-TNGFF

BOOKS 2 READ

Connecting independent readers to independent writers.

Also by Douglas Albert Amos

About the Author

Born in the lush landscapes of Natal, now known as KwaZulu-Natal, the author spent his early years amidst the vibrant culture of South Africa. His career took him to construction sites around the globe, where he built not just structures, but a wealth of experiences. Retirement brought a sense of restlessness, prompting him to dive into the world of writing. With a blend of imagination and expertise, he embarked on a journey to fulfill a lifelong dream.Gratitude fills his heart for the unwavering support he received. The laughter shared with family, the late-night brainstorming sessions with friends, and the encouraging words from colleagues were the pillars of his writing journey. Each moment of support was a beacon, guiding him through the creative process.Studying digital marketing under Max, he absorbed knowledge like a sponge, eager to apply it to his new venture. His upcoming online address will serve as a bridge, connecting him with readers and business associates, ensuring that the bonds he cherishes continue to grow.

Read more at https://www.dougieinterprojects.com.

9 798227 783394